REMEMBERING A WITCH

D0465831

LAUREN CONNOLLY

Visit my website at laurenconnollyromance.com
Cover Designer: Paper and Sage Book Cover Designs
Editor: Jovana Shirley, Unforeseen Editing, www.unforeseenediting.com

ISBN-13: 978-1-949794-04-5

❀ Created with Vellum

For all the women who need second chances.

#JusticeForFenella

FENELLA

*W*hen the deep rumble of a man's chuckle brushes past my ears, ducking behind the nearest large object isn't even a conscious decision.

I don't normally take cover at the sound of laughter. Only I've never heard this particular laugh anywhere other than my dreams. The familiar sound fills my mind with memories that don't belong to me.

As I press my back against the rough bark, I am transported away from the pristine university campus, finding myself surrounded by untamed woods.

Sunlight barely reaches the forest floor, filtering through the tall canopy, stingy about which surfaces the rays illuminate. Small bugs flit about, sparkling when they pass through the light. They add a soft hum to the whistle of the breeze between branches. But all these sights and sounds fall away, overshadowed by the man standing across the clearing from me.

His hair, the vibrant color of a ripe pumpkin, shimmers as if the strands were aflame. A friendly grin shows off a set of charmingly crooked teeth, which parts to let out another roll of chuckles.

I've always loved making Henry laugh.

No, not me, I remind myself.

Marbella made Henry laugh.

I am not Marbella. Henry is not the man I just heard.

They both died long ago.

I press my fingers against my closed eyelids as if that'll clear the phantom image from my mind. After a moment, the wild forest and the handsome man drift away. As the vision dissipates, I drag in a deep breath to calm my racing pulse.

This is what happens when I break with my routine.

I blink my eyes open and find everything is as it should be. The well-manicured, grassy expanse of lawn in the middle of the local university campus stretches out before me. Stray students meander along neatly paved sidewalks, many in shorts and tank tops on this beautiful, sunny day.

Unfortunately, I remain pressed against the tree.

"So, the man sounded like him," I mutter to myself. "That doesn't mean anything."

As I converse with myself, Daisy sits on her haunches, staring up at me. My surprise vision has interrupted her walk, but she is kind enough to wait patiently as I work through my shock.

I pull in another fortifying breath, planning to take a confident step away from my hiding place, spine straight, head held high.

My body betrays me. Instead, I end up pulling the brim of my floppy hat low over my face and peeking around the trunk.

The owner of the laughter is not hard to find. His flaming hair is a beacon, bright and familiar as Henry's.

I retreat. "By all the gods and goddesses, this can't be real. This can't be happening."

Twigs pluck at the back of my long floral dress as I crouch, as if making myself smaller might somehow lessen the magnitude of this situation. Breathing becomes difficult, air stuttering in and out of my lungs, my body forgetting exactly how to absorb oxygen. My mind, despite being well tuned into the magical currents of the world, never expected to meet Henry anywhere other than in my dreams.

He's not Henry, I remind myself.

Not any more than I'm Marbella.

Another memory rises to the surface, this one my own.

"You are the spitting image of her." My mother holds up a *centuries-old painting beside my face, eyes flitting between the image and my teenage scowl with wonder in her expression.*

The heirloom is barely larger than my palm. A portrait of my ancestor, Marbella Henwood. The strongest witch our family has ever laid claim to. A woman who died three hundred years ago.

Discovering I was the reincarnation of a long-ago dead woman has never sat well with me. What is a reincarnation anyway? My mother couldn't give me a good answer. Could never say with utter confidence that I was my own person rather than a copy of one from the past.

I've done my best to forget my odd heritage as I live my life how I see fit.

But my magic doesn't want me to ignore anything. The Henwoods are seers. Prone to visions. A pesky skill that showed up the same time I started using tampons. Dizzy spells would hit me hard moments before my mind fell back hundreds of years to watch short scenes from my ancestor's life.

So, Mom taught me to brew a tea filled with a particular combination of herbs that helped suppress unwanted magical interventions.

But at night, with my mind relaxed in sleep, every so often, Marbella's memories will slip into my dreams. Memories of Henry, the ginger-haired horse breeder she fell in love with.

A man who, it seems, has also been reincarnated.

Mom would claim his appearing here, on a campus in Roanoke, Virginia, where I just happened to be walking my dog, was an act of fate. She has always assured me that, with witches, there's no such thing as coincidences.

But what am I supposed to do with this knowledge?

Even growing up in a household filled with magic, I rejected the idea of my doppelgänger status.

Am I supposed to walk up to this stranger, stick out my hand, and say, "Hello. I'm Fenella Henwood. I've dreamed of you since I was a child. Probably because I'm descended from a line of witches, and I believe that you are the reincarnation of my ancestor's lover"?

In that moment, Daisy's patience runs out. Taking advantage of my distraction, she gives a quick tug, and the leash is out of my hands.

"No! Daisy, come!" My whispered command rushes out low and furious.

She ignores it, dancing away.

"Traitor!"

She wags her tail.

Unlike most dogs, who would use their newfound freedom to bolt, my dog sets out at an almost mockingly slow trot. I could catch up to her easily.

If only I left my hiding spot.

Dread settles in my chest as my furry companion heads straight for the Henry look-alike.

I groan, considering abandoning her out of spite.

If only I didn't love the silly pit bull so much.

One more breath, deep and centering, and I follow her.

I have to clutch my skirt, holding it up so the fabric won't tangle my legs, as I sprint after my dog. With my other hand pressing my hat to my head, I'm sure I look ridiculous. As if sensing my approach, Daisy picks up her pace, beelining for a pair of people, the not-Henry one of them.

The familiar man stands next to a blonde woman who spots Daisy trotting toward them. She lets out a squeak before attempting to hide behind not-Henry in the same way as I just used the tree.

I try not to roll my eyes. With Daisy's cropped ears and muscular body, I know most of the world sees her as the embodiment of aggression. But her lack of a killer instinct is the whole reason she got abandoned.

When I found Daisy in the animal shelter, I knew I couldn't leave without her. There was a force, a push and pull, that existed beyond my physical body. She sat still that day as I lay my palm on her soft head. The expression in her liquid brown eyes was more intelligent than I'd ever expected from any animal.

Finally, you found me, she seemed to say.

And I knew, beyond a doubt, she was my familiar. An animal companion brought to my side by the subtle hint of magic in my veins.

"I'm sorry! She's friendly!" I call out. The classic words of an irresponsible dog owner, but at least I didn't *mean* to let Daisy run loose.

To my surprise, the ginger-haired man crouches low and holds out a hand, inviting Daisy to sidle straight up to him.

Happiness flutters through my chest at the sight, leaving me more breathless than my short sprint.

When I reach them, I'm panting. Unfortunately, with the familiar stranger crouching on the ground, I can't even use the wide brim of my hat to hide my face from him.

"I wasn't paying attention, and she pulled the leash out of my hand. I'm sorry," I breathe the words out with my exhale, watching the top of the man's head as he grins down at my dog.

"Don't worry about it. I …" Whatever he was about to say trails off as he glances up and meets my gaze, surprise slackening his jaw.

Does he feel it too? A strange sense of knowing?

This close, I can see he has the same faded blue irises as Henry. But I also pick up the slight differences between the man of Marbella's memories and this flesh-and-blood figure before me. Not-Henry's carrot hair barely brushes the tops of his ears while original Henry let his locks fall to his shoulders. Not-Henry sports a tame beard, compared to the full growth of original Henry.

Still, underneath it all, the face is the same sharply angled shape.

"I'll see you at the faculty meeting tomorrow." The woman who hid from Daisy practically power-walks away, throwing nervous glances over her shoulder.

Not that my dog has any interest in giving chase. She's too busy getting her belly scratched.

Which brings my gaze to his hands. Long fingers, but this set seems almost soft without the scars of hard work Henry sported. I've stumbled upon an academic, clearly.

And I don't approve of the way my heart beats heavy in my rib cage as I watch not-Henry love on my dog.

The woman had the right idea. It's time to flee.

"Daisy, come here. Leave the nice man alone." I give a

gentle tug on the leash, and my familiar lets out a pathetic groan.

"Have we met before?" Even as the man rises from his crouch, his eyes never leave my face.

Not sure exactly what the truth is, I offer a vague answer. "I'm not a student here. Just enjoy visiting the campus on nice days."

His head tilts, and some phantom pull in my chest begs me to step closer.

But I am my own person, and I shouldn't have to listen to magical urges if I don't want to.

Problem is, I'm too overwhelmed to sift out exactly which wants are mine and which belong to Marbella.

Distance. I need distance.

This time, when I give the leash a firmer tug, Daisy grunts and rolls to her feet, falling in step beside me as I do my best not to look like I'm running away.

"Wait!"

My body listens to him, even as my mind doubts that I should. There's a set of heavy footfalls, and the overwhelming presence of him comes up beside me.

"Do you mind if I walk with you?"

I waver, struggling to come up with a reason to say no, even as I fight the urge to agree to any time I can claim from him. "You don't have somewhere to be?"

A shift at my side draws my eye in time to see him shrug while he smiles down at me. "I might. But, honestly, I can't remember."

For a moment, I'm caught in that murky blue of his irises. There's humor lurking there. So much that it makes me wonder when the last time was that I let myself relax enough to laugh. I'm always worried that letting my guard down means giving my magic a chance to topple me over. But at this moment, there's nothing I want more than to be in on the joke. *His* joke.

"I'm Graham, by the way. Graham Reid." He extends his hand.

"Fenella Henwood." I hesitate a second before returning the gesture, bracing myself for the contact.

I'm not sure what I expected.

Sparks? A clap of thunder? A vision?

None of those things occur. Nothing magical at all in fact.

Still, I find myself not wanting to let go. My dreams—Marbella's memories—consist of sights and sounds. Never touch. His warm skin against mine belongs solely to Graham, no memories of another man overlaying the experience.

We both slacken our grips, but the release is full of hesitation, turning the retreat into an almost-sensual slide of fingers.

We meander side by side, Daisy taking the lead. I study him in my periphery and catch him doing the same. Instead of feeling unnerved, I am fascinated. This casual strolling, under the shade of large oak trees, carries a sense of familiarity. Memories of Marbella and Henry walking together through wilder woods are delicate pencil sketches on tracing paper. If laid over the vivid picture of me next to Graham, the lines match up, but this moment is full of color while the other is pale and insubstantial.

"Do you live here? In Roanoke?" Graham's body holds a thrumming energy that makes me think he's not as comfortable with silence as I am. But I find I don't mind the soothing cadence of his deep, curious voice.

"Yes. I'm a veterinarian at a local clinic." I glance toward Daisy, who has found a beautiful, blooming bush to pee on. My profession is the reason I found her. I happened to be volunteering at the shelter where she was dropped off.

Another not-coincidence.

"A vet," he murmurs. "I have to say, the idea of adopting a pet has never seemed more appealing." He beams down at me.

Warmth pools in my cheeks, and I'm horrified to realize I'm blushing. I *never* blush. I'm too practical to blush. And a man's teasing has never appealed to me before.

"Why are you here?" The question tumbles out of my mouth, born of my confusion and discomfort. And I'm not even sure what I mean by *here*.

Here in this time?

Here in my life?

Here, beside me?

"Well, I work here." Graham continues to watch me instead of the ground in front of his feet. But he doesn't trip or stumble. And his humor doesn't dissipate at my odd question.

"That ... makes sense."

"Does it? Do I look like a professor? Sometimes, I think I should've chosen a more adventurous career. Like a mountain climber. Or a cowboy." Graham grins wide, inviting me to laugh with him. But as his lips part, I see a familiar, slightly crooked set of teeth.

A sliver of my heart aches in recognition, which is tinged with sadness. I rub my chest, soothing the little piece of me that knows this man. Or some version of him at least.

Despite the press of my fingers and a few deep breaths, a surge of magic rushes through my head, and my inner balance tilts. I miss a step, stumbling as I focus inward, pushing away the fragmented visions that threaten to cloud my consciousness.

Damn it. I need my tea.

A sturdy hand cups my elbow while another presses into my lower back. Suddenly, I'm no longer fighting my magic but instead doing a poor job at stifling a pleasurable shiver skittering over my skin.

"You okay, Fenella?"

Say my name again, I want to whisper.

But I don't.

"Long skirt." I shake out the material as if it had tangled around my legs and caused the stumble. Changing the subject and acting in self-preservation, I force myself to put distance between us. "My car is just up here."

We've reached the edge of a visitor parking lot. The smart thing would be to wave and walk away. Instead, I turn to face Graham.

He watches me with eyes that see too much and yet nothing of the truth.

What am I supposed to do with this man?

Can I keep him?

"Would you want to get coffee sometime? I just moved here at the beginning of this semester. I've been looking for someone to show me around." Graham offers an entreating smile, even as his cheeks go ruddy. He's an appealing mixture of confidence and chagrin.

Whatever the universe's plans are for the two of us, I'm losing the battle against them.

"All right. I'll give you my number." I hold my hand out for his phone.

He pats his pockets and then searches through his bag. His hands come up empty. "Damn. Must've left it in my office. Let me just …" Another dive of his fingers retrieves a pen, but then he resumes frantic searching. "I know I have something to write on. It can't all be student papers," he mutters to himself and then clamps the pen in his teeth in order to use both hands to search.

The whole display makes me want to laugh. Instead, I step in close enough to make him pause, slide the pen from his mouth, and reach down to clasp one of his hands. The ink shows up beautifully against his pale skin. I use slow strokes to write out my name and phone number. Then, not quite ready to let go, I trace a simple vine around my contact information.

Realizing what I've done, I drop his hand and offer the pen back.

Graham accepts it, letting the tip of his thumb brush mine.

"I'll call you, Fenella." He stares down at me with an excited smile, as if I'm somehow fascinating to him.

I'm certain this brief interaction has turned my orderly life upside down, and I can feel the pressure of a denied vision building up in the back of my skull. I need to get away.

Even if standing here holds a sense of contentment I never expected.

"Good-bye, Graham."

The second I say the words, my heart crushes under the weight of a mysterious sorrow.

2

GRAHAM

SIX MONTHS LATER

I slowly rise from the dream, the time between sleeping and waking connected by the face I see when my eyes open.

Fenella is lying in the bed next to me, body relaxed in slumber. I keep still, not ready to rouse her just yet. She's an early riser, normally halfway through breakfast before my alarm has even gone off. Catching her still snoozing is a rare treat, and I enjoy my chance to watch her completely relaxed.

Not that me staring at her is unusual. One of my favorite activities is watching my girlfriend; I find every bit of her fascinating. The way her slender lips take their time curling into a smile that is worth the wait. The way her nose scrunches when I say something she doesn't want to find funny but secretly does. The way her fingers dance around when she's forgotten what she meant to be doing.

Fenella has held my attention since the first day I saw her six months ago, chasing her dog across campus.

Actually, I was intrigued with her long before that. But that's bound to happen when you dream of the same woman for years.

I prop my head in my hand, staring down at Fenella and admitting that the person I occasionally see while I'm asleep is slightly different than the woman next to me. Dream-Fenella is always younger and dressed in old-fashioned clothes. Like an Amish version of my girlfriend.

Maybe I spotted Fenella at a renaissance fair when I was a teenager, and her beautiful face with its dark lashes and tilted nose imprinted on my subconscious.

Whatever chance meeting happened in the past, at least this time, I was smart enough not to let her walk away.

A spear of sunlight spills over the bottom of the windowsill, sneaking through a crack in the curtains and caressing Fenella's sloping neck. Her skin glows with the light, and I consider kissing the spot.

But she needs her sleep. Long hours and stressful surgeries have stained the area under her eyes with exhaustion. Her work ethic, the devotion she has to helping every animal that shows up at her office, is one of many reasons I'm captivated by her. Every moment I spend with this woman just makes me want to extend our time together.

More than once, I've found myself studying the window display of a jewelry shop, considering what a diamond might look like on Fenella's left hand.

Unfortunately, our relationship has one major obstacle I've yet to find a way to overcome.

Fenella is normal.

Well, kind of. Actually, she's silly and magnificent and odd. She colors in intricate mandalas to deal with stress, and she makes elaborately decorated cupcakes on her days off. She gasps out loud as she's reading suspense books and has an entire closet dedicated to the storage of seasonal decorations. When I've spent hours hunched over, grading my students' tests, she commands me to lie facedown on the couch and then uses her strong, dancing fingers to knead away all the tension in my shoulders.

Fenella is an extremely intoxicating, perfectly normal version of odd.

What my girlfriend has never done is shown the slightest interest in the mythical or magical.

One day, I was watching Harry Potter when she walked into the room.

She stayed for less than a minute of the movie before snorting, muttering, "Yeah, right," and strolling back to the kitchen.

Fenella clearly has no interest in or time for magic.

Which makes the fact that I'm a magical being a hard topic to broach.

I reach my hand out to trace over her shoulder, stopping just before I make contact, remembering my decision to let her sleep. Instead, I extend my arm further. I'm just close enough to brush the tip of my finger against the wilting leaf of a plant on her bedside table. Fenella is notoriously bad at remembering to water her plants.

Luckily, she has me around to keep them all from dying.

The magic that has imbued my entire being since I was a kid always settles in my palms, occasionally pushing at my fingertips in a silent request to be let out. In the hush of the morning, I answer, letting the energy spill from the surface of my skin to the waxy green leaves. Before, the plant hung in dejected defeat. After my caressing, the stems regain their strength, the tips of the vines rising proud and healthy in their colorful pot.

With a content sigh, I let the tingle of the power calm again, enjoying the sensation similar to the feeling of having stretched a sore muscle.

Something, maybe my movement or my breath, upsets Fenella's light sleep. I should curse myself for disturbing her, but I find I don't regret the blunder when her unfocused eyes come to rest on my face. A lovely smile blooms as she stares up at me.

"Good morning, beautiful," I whisper, kissing the tilted tip of her nose.

Fenella's hands reach for me, fingers sliding along my waist before diving under my shirt, nails running over my back in a sensual tease that has me groaning. I bury my head in her neck, catching a faint trace of her rose-water perfume.

As I kiss the spot touched by sunlight, she presses her body against mine, making me want to wake up early every morning. We wrap ourselves around one another, lazy movements filled with delicious promise.

My lips reach the corner of her mouth just as my palm cups one of her butt cheeks. Fenella turns her head away, even as she arches into me.

"I've got morning breath," she groans.

I chuckle and gently bite her earlobe.

Her hands drop to the waistband of my boxer briefs, knuckles brushing against my hardness. "I need you to wake me up," she murmurs with a teasing lilt in her voice.

My laugh gets strangled by a moan as she frees me and slings her leg over my waist. Fenella always wears a large T-shirt to bed. That and nothing else.

Even though I want to bury myself in her immediately, I hold myself back. Her skin is hot and soft as I trace my fingers down her stomach, finding the springy curls that let me know I've almost reached gold. Fenella pants in my ear when I part her folds, firmly pressing on her clit and then massaging the secret spot with the pad of my finger.

When I'm sure she's wet and ready for me, I position the

head of my cock at her entrance. I take her slow, a groan pulled from my chest by her warm grip.

Seeking a better angle, I shift to sit up, pressing my back against the headboard and clasping her hips as she straddles me. We rock together deliberately, in no hurry for the paradise to end.

Fenella rises and falls over me, letting her hands act as curious wanderers traversing my chest, climbing my neck. The soft caress of her fingers turns into an erotic bite as she drags her nails along my scalp.

"Do that again," I command, reveling in the way she explores my body.

"So demanding," Fenella pretends to scold, even as she repeats her action.

I grunt and stare up at her, trying to figure out how I got so lucky. Fenella is the woman of my dreams—literally—and she's gazing down at me with a hazy-eyed expression that I've learned means her release is close.

My fingers slide to the tight bundle of nerves that contain her pleasure, earning me a gasp and nails digging into my shoulders.

"Graham …" Fenella trails off, but the reverent tone she uses to utter my name slams into my chest, clutching my heart, battering my lungs, and forcing words past my lips without consulting my brain.

"I love you."

Her lusty expression morphs into shock that just as quickly dissolves with a broken cry, her entire body clenching and shaking with her climax.

As Fenella rides through the sensations, I pull her tight against my chest, one arm wrapped around her waist and my other hand guiding her head to rest under my chin. I hold her as she breaks apart and pray that when she's knitted back together, her first action won't be to retreat from me.

Fenella slowly relaxes in my arms, and I try not to crush her with my embrace. Any second, I expect her to pull away.

When she finally moves, the maneuver is a tantalizing roll of her hips. I'm still hard inside her, my body begging for its own release.

A soft touch against my neck gives me hope. She's kissing me. She's tightening her inner muscles around me.

Fenella keeps her body pressed close to mine as she gently coaxes my orgasm to the surface. Soon, I'm the one letting out broken cries as ecstasy courses through my nerve endings.

We stay locked together, even as I go liquid, sliding down the headboard, practically a puddle of satisfied man.

Definitely the best morning I've ever had.

Until Fenella fulfills my fears and pulls away.

She untangles herself from me, rising from the bed without a word, not meeting my eyes. As I sit up, she slips out the bedroom door. The muffled sound of a shower running echoes down the hall.

I mutter a string of curses, collapsing back on the bed. Every foul word is directed at myself.

I love you? In the middle of sex?

Most people would think having a PhD in biology would be a good indication of my intelligence. Maybe I should've focused my dissertation on how not to fuck up a relationship with my perfect woman. Clearly, I need to do more research on the topic.

The jingle of dog tags alerts me to Daisy's approach. She wanders her way into the room, hops up on the bed, and stares down at me with eyes that seem too insightful for a canine. After a moment, she lets out a doggy huff that sounds a lot like, *You fucked up, dude.*

"Yeah, yeah. I know."

"Know what?" Fenella asks as she strolls back into the

room, wearing only a towel, wet hair pulled up in a messy bun on top of her head.

I tug a blanket over my waist, covering the evidence of what the sight of her does to me.

"I know"—I search my brain for an answer other than the truth—"that Daisy wants a walk. I can take her. I don't teach until ten."

"Thank you," Fenella says over her shoulder.

Then, she drops her towel, and I have to bite my fist to stifle a groan.

Acting the voyeur, I watch my naked girlfriend rifle through her drawers until she finds and pulls on a black sports bra and matching set of cotton panties. I mourn each expanse of skin lost until she finishes with a set of navy scrubs. Even in the shapeless outfit, Fenella is still beautiful.

Half of me wants to pull her back into the bed and pleasure her until she can't help but love me as much as I love her. The other half wants to take the words back, so she has no reason to think I'm pressuring her into more than she's ready for.

"You don't teach on Mondays this semester, right?" Her question pulls me out of my dueling thoughts.

"No. Just office hours."

Finally, for the first time since I uttered the relationship-altering statement, Fenella meets my gaze.

"Would you want to go on a hike and camp out Sunday night?"

A small amount of tension in my chest eases. Planning a weekend together seems like a good sign.

"Yes. Definitely. I would love that."

Fenella's eyes drop at my use of that stupid, truthful word.

Shit.

But she doesn't retract the invite.

"All right. Just you and me. I thought I'd drop Daisy off at my mom's." We both glance at the dog, who has curled up in the warm spot Fenella left when she climbed out of bed. "She's too lazy to spend all day walking."

"Good call. Not sure I could carry her very far."

We share a grin, and happiness tingles through my limbs when Fenella settles on the edge of the bed beside me. With an almost-hesitant hand, she reaches up to brush a thumb over my beard and then leans in for a swift kiss.

Before I can prolong the affectionate gesture, Fenella breaks off and stands.

"I have to head into work." She pauses just before disappearing, fingers clutching the doorjamb as she glances back. "When I … when I go to my mom's, would you want to come?"

Despite the fact that Fenella's mother lives just outside of town, I've never met the woman in the six months I've been dating her daughter. This invitation holds almost as much weight as her returning my declaration of love.

"Yes! I would lo—" I cough to cover my stumble, careful not to make the same mistake twice. "Like … I would *like* to come with you."

Fenella nods, staring past me as if she's deep in thought. "And then we'll go hiking."

"Then, we'll go hiking," I agree.

"In the woods." The words are just a fleeting murmur as she leaves me.

3

FENELLA

Her basket is half-full of dogwood bark when she hears a man's voice. This far into the woods, she did not expect to cross paths with anyone.

Worried about what sort of man might have made the long hike, she uses the cover of trees and mid-morning shadows to conceal herself as she approaches where she heard the stranger speak.

"You're a lovely lady. I hate to hurt you." His words send a fearful chill trickling down her spine.

Who is he going to hurt?

She should run home for help, but the cabin is half a morning's walk. Even running would take more than an hour there and back. The man will have plenty of time to injure whoever this woman is.

She won't allow it.

She searches the ground for some sort of weapon.

Hefting a heavy branch in her hand, she moves toward the man. From years spent scouring the woods for herbs, she has mastered the skill of passing soundlessly.

"I shall be quick, I swear."

Dread pools low in her gut at the casual words. She can guess what he means by them.

The deep voice came from just behind the next tree. She holds her breath while cautiously peering around the bend. Luck is on her side, as the man's back is turned to her hiding spot. Unfortunately, she cannot find his intended victim.

The man stands on the edge of a tiny clearing, a large enough break in the canopy that sunlight spills down without hindrance. With everything lit so well, she can't imagine where the girl might be concealed. The man himself, while tall, is not very broad. Like a stalk of corn. His lithe body shouldn't be large enough to obstruct the view of a grown woman.

"You should know, you're going to make a sturdy fence."

A fence? *She struggles to understand this newest threat against a woman she cannot locate. Her eyes lock on the man, hoping his body language might give some sort of hint as to where his victim is.*

But he looks at no one.

In fact, he seems to be fully facing a tree, his hand braced against the trunk. He doesn't even try to search around the other side of it, as if a girl might be crouched there. Instead, his fingers trail over the bark.

"Still, it's a shame. I really do prefer to find wood that's already fallen."

Her mind makes quick work of the situation, and the sudden realization of the truth has her throwing caution to the wind.

"A tree?" *she exclaims in disbelief.*

The man whirls at the sound of her voice, revealing the ax in his hand and a dumbfounded expression on his face. She steps into the clearing to make sure, still keeping her distance.

"Pardon me, miss?"

"I thought you were about to murder a woman! Have you been talking to a tree this whole time?"

The scarlet flush that spreads across his cheeks is answer enough. She finds herself laughing, the giggles spilling out of her with abandon.

The life her family lives is not an easy one, trying to carve out an existence in the wilds of the colonies. Therefore, she appreciates every humorous moment to be found.

Some men might become offended at a woman laughing at them, but this fellow grins along with her. As she catches her breath, she lets her eyes trail over his form. Though pale as milk, he is clearly a man used to hard labor with corded muscles and a sure hold on his tool. His hair falls to his shoulders in flaming waves. She wonders what it might be like to comb her fingers through it.

"In my defense, I believed that only the tree was listening." He continues to smile at her. "Might I ask the name of my surprise audience?"

Stifling the tail end of her chuckles, she offers a shallow curtsy. "I'm Marbella Henwood. And you, sir?"

"Henry Reid, at your service," he responds with a deep bow.

"Seems to me you are more in service of that tree. Why exactly were you conversing with it?"

His blush grows darker, and she enjoys the way the color clashes with his hair.

Still, he clears his throat and answers, "Everything seems more alive on these lands. I only seek to soften the death blow I must deal and hope that the life that fills these woods understands my actions."

The bare honesty rings in her bones, drawing her farther into the clearing.

She likes this strange man. And so, she feels the strong urge to tease him.

"Dear me, it seems we are at odds then."

His smile falters. "How so?"

"You see"—she moves another step closer—"I came here to save an innocent, and I am still fixing to do so."

His thick beard twitches. "Ah, well, that is noble of you, Miss

Henwood. But I need wood. One of these trees is coming down today. It might as well be this one."

"I am sorry, Mr. Reid. But I cannot let you do that." She is now in front of him, close enough to admire the faded blue of his irises.

"And why is that?"

Marbella leans back against the rough bark, tilting her head up to gift Henry with a winning smile. "Because this tree is not the same as all the others." She reaches forward, not caring the slightest about impropriety as she fixes the rumpled collar of his shirt.

"How does it differ?" He brings his hand up, wrapping long fingers around her wrist. But he does not remove her hand. Instead, Henry gently guides her palm to his lips, brushing a light kiss over her bare knuckles.

"Did you not know?" Her voice has gone light as a spring breeze, and her lips tilt in teasing.

Henry raises one ginger brow, waiting for her to continue, the corner of his mouth curving.

Marbella smiles wider. "This is our tree."

When a memory ends, I can never transition into normal sleep. For some reason, after living a time as Marbella, my body demands I wake up.

My eyelids flutter open, and I stare at the shadowy ceiling, needing a minute to figure out which bedroom I'm in. Graham's solid, warm body lies beside me, but that's not really a clue. Slowly, I realize he's on my left, which means I'm on the right side of the bed. We're in Graham's bedroom. I always sleep on the side closest to the door. Less likely to wake him when I get up to pee in the middle of the night.

My minuscule bladder demands I use that advantage now.

Slipping out from under the covers, I move to the door, only to pause and glance back at the bed. Graham sleeps on his stomach, hugging his pillow, the sheets bunched at his waist to reveal a large expanse of naked back. His skin is pale, soaking in the scant light given off by the digital clock on his bedside table. I want to sprawl over him, cover every vulnerable inch. Press our skin together until we've marked each other permanently.

The strength of my longing has me scurrying from the room.

I navigate the townhouse in the dark. After using the bathroom, I veer off toward the kitchen to fill a glass with water at the sink. The marble counter is cold, even through my shirt, as I lean against it, sipping my drink. Considering the memory.

This isn't the first time I've lived through the moment Marbella and Henry met. But the fact that the experience arose again tonight, the day before the autumn equinox, feels like a sign. As if the universe or Marbella or maybe even the spirit of Mabon is trying to show me that I'm on the right path.

Of course, none of them wants to tell me exactly where this trail leads.

4

GRAHAM

"What did you do to your leg?" Fenella's glare somehow mixes both anger and concern. She directs it at the woman hobbling toward us from the front door of the house we just pulled up to.

Virginia Henwood smirks.

She shares her daughter's lovely sculpted cheekbones and tilt-tipped nose. The wrinkles that scatter from the corner of her eyes draw the gaze to her warm expression. The small markers of her age deepen when she grins wide at her daughter's scolding.

"I fell," Virginia offers before pulling Fenella in close for a kiss on the cheek. She doesn't bother to explain any further before turning to face me. "And this must be Graham." She clasps the hand I offer in two of hers, making the handshake feel more like an embrace. "I don't know why you've been hiding him. He's handsome."

A blush rises hot in my face, and I doubt she'll continue to think I'm good-looking as my red cheeks clash with my hair.

"Yes, Graham is extremely attractive, and I'm lucky to

have him in my life. Don't change the subject. What do you mean by, *you fell*? Off of what? Why didn't you call me?"

As Fenella interrogates her mother, all the warmth from my embarrassed face transfers to my chest with a content glow. Just because she sped through the compliments doesn't mean the sincerity in them was any less.

Fenella is not much of a talker. She never fills comfortable silences with chatter. When she speaks, there's normally an important point to her words. Once that point is conveyed, she is happy to settle back into silence.

I've learned not to expect affectionate words. My girlfriend is prone to long, meaningful gazes or a tender brush of her fingers along my lower back.

The fact that I was the first to say *I love you* was no surprise.

What hurt was her not speaking the words back.

But now, at least, I know she feels lucky to have me in her life.

My hopes about the point of this trip solidify.

Fenella is going to tell me she loves me.

Only I'm sure she just wants to make it special. Someone as intelligent as her is not going to blurt those important words out in the middle of sex like an extra bit of dirty talk. Fenella is going to take me out to the woods where we'll set up a comfortable camp, and then under the expansive night sky, full of endless stars, she will tell me how she loves me too.

"I was just trying to reach some of the top branches."

While I've been reeling from the first part of Fenella's statement, her mother has been answering the second half. Virginia gestures to a tree in the middle of her front yard. The whole house is surrounded by towering oaks, the home existing within its own forest. However, the one Virginia indicates only grows as tall as the second story. Branches spread out far and thick before narrowing to round, waxy leaves.

"I don't think the birds care how high you get the feeders, Mom."

"It just looks so bottom heavy. And today is all about balance." Virginia limps to her front porch, seemingly unbothered by the cast on her leg. "But you're right. I should've called you. You're much better at climbing than I am." The woman turns back, a cardboard box in her arms and a hopeful smile on her lips.

Fenella lets out a sigh and then brushes my sleeve with her fingers. "Could you let Daisy out and grab the gifts?"

A moment later, the pit bull is galloping around the yard, snuffling in the few leaves that have started to fall, and I'm watching my girlfriend expertly scale a tree as I clutch a Tupperware container and a pumpkin. The sight of her mounting each branch, navigating the limbs with skill, is strangely erotic. Fenella is in complete control of every move she makes.

"A pumpkin! Is that for me?" Virginia sets her box down to hold out eager hands.

"I grow them." I offer by way of explanation as I pass off the beautifully shaped gourd.

Delight sparkles in the woman's gaze.

"I told you she'd love it," Fenella calls out from her perch. "You should see his garden, Mom. Graham can grow anything."

"Anything?" Virginia examines me, and I get the sense she sees right through my normal human act, straight to my magical core.

"Fenella made apple cider cupcakes." I hold up the other gift, trying to take the attention off my exceptionally green thumb.

"Someone needs to hand me the bird feeders."

"Here. You're much taller than me." Virginia sets down the pumpkin to take the cupcakes, freeing my hands to help.

When I grab the box and head toward the tree, I realize the bird feeders are all pinecones covered in peanut butter and bird seed. Little bits of twine wrap around the tips and form loops to hang them. I dangle one from my finger, admiring the quaint fall ornament.

"Graham?" Fenella stares down at me, a smile teasing at the corner of her lips.

"Sorry. Just looking." I reach my long arm up, and our skin brushes as she hooks a finger around the twine.

As we repeat the process, I can't help staring at Fenella. She looks like a regal wood nymph, surrounded by the leaves, effortlessly balancing on each branch, her fingers nimble as she hangs the pinecones from different twigs.

When the box is empty, I place it on the ground and reach up to help Fenella descend from her perch. The soft curves of her body press against mine as she lets herself fall into my arms. Instead of immediately letting go, I clutch her closer, pressing my nose into the dark mass of rose-scented hair and begging the universe that she won't disappear into the forest like a mischievous sprite.

I don't think my heart would survive the loss.

FENELLA

I scrub our dishes from breakfast and peer out the kitchen window, watching Graham trot down Mom's front drive with Daisy beside him on a leash. A shuffle and clunk alert me to my mother's approach.

"Are you sure you're fine to watch Daisy?" I ask.

"Oh, stop. It's just a sprain. I'm not bedridden. I'm

perfectly capable of opening the back door to let her out. And she's too smart to wander."

One of the rickety wooden chairs at the table creaks, and I glance over my shoulder to watch her settle herself. When our eyes meet, a confused frown flickers over a mouth made for smiling.

"Why are you taking him out tonight, of all nights? Not that I'm saying you *have* to spend Mabon with me. But ... we do have traditions."

A tinge of dread mixing uncomfortably with excitement attempts to curdle the scrambled eggs in my stomach.

"He looks like Henry."

My words are met with silence. I shut off the water, grab a towel, and turn to face my mother as I dry my hands. Her puzzled expression tells me she doesn't remember the name.

That shouldn't be a surprise. It never meant as much to her as it did to me.

"He looks *exactly* like Marbella's Henry."

Understanding flares in her eyes like a struck match. "You mean ..."

I fiddle with the towel, weaving it through my fingers. Then, I tell her everything. She only knew I'd been dating a man named Graham who taught at the local university. Until this moment, I've kept all mentions of reincarnation to myself.

"I thought ... well, I don't know what I thought. That the universe was demanding I interact with him maybe? But he's not ... Graham is different than Henry. And I couldn't help ..." A sudden pressure pushes behind my eyes, and I bury my face in the dish towel, hating the idea of giving in to tears.

"Oh, baby girl." The chair groans again, and a set of strong, familiar arms wraps me in a comforting embrace. She squeezes me tight before leaning back against the counter beside me.

Mom can always tell when I have more to say.

I suck in a deep, steadying breath and then let it out slow with my next words. "Graham told me he loves me."

"And you don't?" She keeps her voice free of any judgment.

"That's the thing. I think I *do* love him." My teeth dig into my bottom lip before I push on. "But I can't tell him. Not when, every day, I feel like I'm lying to him." *When I'm not even sure these feelings are mine*, I add silently.

Her warm palm rubs calming circles on my back, and I'm reminded of all the problems I've brought to my mother in the last thirty-four years. None have ever felt this important.

"You're telling him tonight? About your powers? About Marbella and Henry?"

Nerves tighten my shoulders, and my mom lets her hand fall away.

"I have a plan to figure out if he even wants to know. And if he does, I'll tell him." I nod to myself, ignoring the tight knot in my stomach.

"And if he's fine with it? Will you accept his love?" She can't keep the hope out of her voice.

I twist the towel in my hands. "I need to know what happened. With Marbella and Henry."

"Ah." The understanding in her tone draws my gaze. "So, that's why you asked for those." She nods toward a bundle on the table, one I need to tuck into my backpack before we leave. "And why you're taking him tonight. Why you're going to the woods."

I tilt my head in a combination of a nod and a shake. "Not just any woods. I'm taking him to where it all started."

5

GRAHAM

*F*enella takes the lead on the trail, and I'm happy to act as the caboose. For one, I get to admire her round butt and toned legs as she climbs over roots and navigates the dirt path. But also, it's better if she sets the pace.

Surrounded as we are by nature, pure energy thrums through my veins. I'm barely able to keep from running through the forest just for the sheer joy of it.

Plus, I'm practically giddy from this morning. Breakfast with Virginia—as Fenella's mom insisted I call her—went great. She didn't have the look of a woman who pitied a man about to be broken up with by her daughter. The entire time, Virginia grinned at me, told embarrassing stories about my girlfriend as a moody teenager, and plied me with heaps of scrambled eggs and bacon, claiming I'd need my strength for the trek.

But I could've had a simple slice of toast for breakfast and still have felt supercharged. The plants themselves nourish me.

I let my touch trail over bark and leaves, reveling in the thrum of power. Tendrils of magic snake out from the tips of my fingers, and I'm confident this area of the woods will likely be the last to descend into the chill of autumn.

In late September, the Blue Ridge Mountains continue to glitter green. But when fall comes to the forest, the mountain sides will fade into an elaborate quilt of oranges and reds.

After a few hours and a long ascent, we break through the trees. I'm briefly disoriented by the dramatic shift of views. A moment ago, I could barely see ten feet in front of me, surrounded as we were by the dense foliage. Now, I can gaze for miles.

"McAfee Knob." Fenella smiles at me over her shoulder. Then, she slides her backpack off and walks unencumbered onto the large rock outcrop.

The ledge is spacious, and we're not the only ones who've made the climb. A middle-aged man sits cross-legged with his eyes closed, seeming to meditate. A pair of girls laughs and takes turns snapping photos of each other with the vast expanse of woods acting as a glorious background. Fenella maneuvers around them, getting closer to the edge than I find entirely comfortable.

My bag hits the ground beside hers, and I follow.

Lucky for me, I'm not scared of heights or else I might hyperventilate at the drop-off. Fenella stands still, mere feet from the edge, gazing out at the rolling mountains covered in their wooded blankets.

"This is amazing," I speak quietly to keep from startling her.

Fenella tucks a loose strand of hair behind her ear that the strong breeze tugged free. "I always forget how far you can see."

I wrap an arm around her shoulders, and she leans into me. The beauty of the moment intensifies my need to connect with her. To know that we aren't temporary.

The wind picks up around us as I tilt her chin for my

searching kiss. She tastes like the peanut butter granola bar she had as a snack, and hints of her rose-water perfume tickle my nose. I breathe in deep, letting my arm fall to her waist so I can pull her warm body flush against mine.

When we break apart, both of us are grinning.

We settle down farther from the edge, eating lunch in the warmth of the sun.

One of the girls who was taking selfies sidles up to us.

"That was really sweet." She waves to the spot where we kissed. "I ... well, I took a picture. Accidentally." The girl blushes as her friend snickers a few feet away. But she soldiers on when Fenella gives her one of those slow, kind smiles my girlfriend is a master of. "Anyway, if you give me your number, I can text it to you. It's just ... super cute." She shrugs.

"Yes." The word is out of my mouth before Fenella can answer. Whatever her thoughts, I want that picture with an intense burning.

I rattle off my phone number, and soon, I'm staring down at perfection.

Well, my version of it anyway.

The image of the woman I love in the circle of my arms with forest-covered mountains stretching far behind us makes a perfect background on my phone. I make a mental note to get it printed and framed, so I can display it in my cluttered office.

After gathering our trash, we plunge back into the woods.

An hour passes before Fenella stops, turning to me. "Do you mind if I take us off the trail?"

I shrug. "If you know where you're going, be my guest."

We leave the path behind.

The trees close in tighter around us, but Fenella doesn't hesitate. She navigates the forest as easily as strolling through the university campus.

I enjoy the way nature embraces us and take the idea of *leave no trace behind* to the next level by allowing my power to heal the small destructions left in our wake. Twigs reconnect to their branches, and the plants we crush under our hiking boots stand tall again just seconds later.

After a time, I wonder if Fenella has led us in a circle. The trees and rocks and even the moss begin to feel familiar. As if I've been this way before.

But that can't be right.

I was born and spent most of my life in New Hampshire. Occasionally, I went on trips out of the state but never to Virginia, much less Roanoke. The first time I ever visited the state was for my job interview at the university. Actually, I was interviewing for three different positions across the county at the time. But something pulled me here. Maybe the fact that my great-grandparents had lived in the area, and I was hungry for some family history.

But if I'm being honest, there was just a feeling when I drove around the town that this was *my* place.

And now, this section of woods has the same tug. As if this space knows me. As if it's glad I've returned.

"I thought we'd set up camp here," Fenella says a moment before we step into a clearing.

The break in the trees isn't large, maybe the size of a townhouse's backyard, but it's flat, and it imbues an innate sense of comfort.

I walk the perimeter before answering, coming to a halt next to a particularly beautiful oak. The trunk has gotten fat with age, and it towers overhead. When I press my hand to the bark, a curious tingle fills my entire body.

I grin over my shoulder, only to find Fenella staring at me, wide-eyed.

As if she's seen a ghost.

FENELLA

The sun hasn't disappeared completely, but it's sunk low enough that the light from the fire is helpful. I add a larger branch to the blaze, enjoying the crackles and pops that accompany the flames gnawing away at the wood.

You are just putting off the inevitable, a traitorous voice whispers in the back of my mind.

I wonder if it is Marbella speaking to me through the centuries, finally able to communicate now that I've ventured into this special place on one of the most magical times of the year.

It would be rude to force an unwanted truth on him when we haven't even eaten yet, I reason, glancing at our foil-pouch dinners.

There's no response from the phantom voice.

Graham spreads a blanket on the ground close enough to the fire that the warmth will reach us, even when the chill of the night descends. Then, with a groan, he settles down, propping his back against a large, mossy rock.

"I need to get out more," he declares before grinning at me.

Despite my nerves, I respond with a smile, "I'm sorry. I didn't mean to wear you out."

He scoffs, "Worn out? I just need a minute to rest. Then, I'll have all the energy in the world for any other camping activities you have in mind." The tone of his voice makes it clear exactly what activities Graham would like us to get up to.

I turn my head back to our food, not sure what expression is showing on my face. There's nothing I'd like more than to christen my tiny tent with him. The idea of being intimate with Graham under the stars is even more appealing.

But is it true intimacy if there are still lies hovering between us?

When I judge the food to be done, I carefully remove the hot foil bundles from the fire and settle beside Graham, offering him one. Steam billows as we crack the makeshift cooking apparatuses open and dig into the carrots and potatoes with sporks.

"Holy hell, babe. This is delicious. I didn't know campfire food could taste so good." He shoves another bite in his mouth and lets out an appreciative moan.

I chuckle. "A long day of hiking makes anything taste good. Well, that, and a whole lot of butter."

Graham reaches out to give my knee an affectionate squeeze, and warmth floods my veins that has nothing to do with the hot food or the crackling fire.

Unfortunately, our meal ends far too quickly.

I busy myself cleaning up, but there's not enough involved to fill even five minutes. Soon, I'm back to feeding wood to the flames.

My boyfriend, normally prone to chatting, is strangely quiet. As if he knows there's something I need to say.

With a sigh, I give in, moving to sit cross-legged on the blanket, back to the fire, facing Graham. He watches expectantly, not pushing me to talk sooner than I'm ready.

I love this man. And the idea of us walking out of these woods and him never wanting to see me again is what keeps sticking the words in my throat.

After a definitive throat clearing, I force the first bit out. "You said you love me."

His beard twitches as he dips his head in a nod.

A small bit of my anxiety eases. At least he's not taking the words back. Yet.

I slip my fingers into the back pocket of my jeans and pull

out a folded piece of notebook paper. After smoothing it out on my knee, I risk meeting Graham's gaze again.

"I'm going to ask you some questions. They are all hypothetical, but I would like you to give me an honest answer." I watch confusion wrinkle his brow. "Can you do that?"

"Yeah, Fenny, I can do that." He pulls out a nickname I pretend I don't like while, deep down, I relish the affectionate tone he uses whenever he says it.

I make a show of looking down at my paper, as if I don't have every word memorized. "What would you say if I told you I was in witness protection?"

Now, Graham is the one coughing, as if needing to clear his throat. "Are you?" He chokes out.

I glare. "Hypothetically."

He still looks baffled, but then his face slowly clears as he takes a moment to think it over. After a few minutes pass, he meets my eyes, and I see nothing but sincerity.

"I would tell you, you shouldn't have told me."

My heart grows heavy and uncomfortable in my chest, but he keeps talking, "Because, as far as I know, you're not supposed to tell anyone, even your family. That the more people who know, the greater risk there is to you. And I would never want you to get hurt."

My anxiety lessens, and I have to stifle a grin. A half-smile still peeks out, and Graham's eyes land on my mouth. I ignore the urge to throw my questions aside and straddle him.

This is important.

"All right, next question. What would you say if I told you I planned to move to the Alaskan tundra to study polar bears?"

He can't help smirking and shaking his head at that, but he still doesn't throw out a useless, joking response. "I would say that the Alaskan tundra doesn't have many universities for a biology professor to teach in and ask if you'd consider living in a city like Anchorage and taking a few extended trips to the tundra for your studies."

The earnestness rocks me. "You'd move to Alaska with me?"

Graham tilts his head. "Hypothetically."

I nod, steeling myself for the next not-at-all hypothetical question. "What would you say if I told you I was a witch?"

Graham flinches slightly, and my breath comes faster.

"You mean, if you thought you were a witch or if you actually were one?"

"The second." I decide to stick as close to the truth as I can.

He tugs on his ear for a minute. "What kind of witch?"

I'm not surprised this scenario has follow-up questions. The other two would at least seem feasible to a human. "A relatively harmless one. Some minor powers that I don't use too often."

He smiles, clearly thinking this is some kind of get-to-know-your-partner game. "I'd ask you about your powers and if you could show me any of them."

"But you would still love a witch?" I try to keep the desperation out of my voice.

"I have no problem loving a witch. Especially if that witch is you."

Heat stains my cheeks, and I hurriedly blurt out my next ridiculous question, "What would you say if I told you I was actually sixty years old, not thirty-four?"

Graham lets out a bark of laughter and then shoves his fist against his mouth when I scowl at him.

After a moment though, his humor fades away to a frown, and I wonder what he's thinking.

"I would be … sad."

"Sad?" I grapple with a hint of offense on behalf of the fictional sixty-year-old me.

Graham drags his long fingers through his hair. "Yeah. That's twenty-six years I thought I had with you. Just … gone."

I swallow hard, the sweetness of that statement too much to handle without getting slightly choked up. "I'm not. Sixty, that is."

His mouth curves, and his pale blue eyes go soft. "Glad to hear it."

I fiddle with my paper, trying to maintain the same innocently curious tone I've used with all the fake questions. "What if I told you I saw your face in a dream before we ever met?"

He doesn't respond immediately, and I stare at my long list of made-up questions as I let him think over an answer. I consider how many more false scenarios I'll have to lay out before admitting the truth becomes less frightening.

"Did you? Did you see me in a dream?" Graham's ragged tone shocks me into glancing up at him.

There's no humor or discomfort on his face. Now, he stares at me as if ravenous.

"We're dealing in hypotheticals," I whisper.

He doesn't take his eyes off me. "I'd tell you I dreamed about you too." As he speaks, he leans across the blanket toward me, and I'm confident that if I tried to run away, he would chase after me. "Not every night, but often enough. Ever since I was a teenager." He pauses at my gasp but then repeats his question, "Did you see me in a dream?"

"No."

Graham sits back hard, his face stark and vulnerable as if I slapped him.

"I dreamed about Henry," I clarify.

Confusion creases Graham's forehead, and I feel my own rising to the surface.

"And Marbella," I say, sure her name will mean something to him.

"Marbella?"

He's had dreams like me but not of our past selves?

I reach for my backpack and draw out the bundle my mother gathered for me. From it, I pull the palm-sized portrait of my centuries-old relative and offer it to Graham. As his wild eyes flick from the painting to my face, I know he is seeing the clear resemblance.

"Who is Marbella?"

"She's my ancestor. She died in the early seventeen hundreds." I brace myself for whatever reaction might come at my next words. "I'm a reincarnation of her. Which is likely possible because I am descended from a long line of witches."

"Witches?" he breathes the word, eyes wide.

And, suddenly, I find myself doing something quite out of character. I begin to ramble, "The Henwoods have all been witches, going back centuries. There're multiple kinds of witches, but my family is mainly seers. You know, past, present, future. I was never very good at understanding what I saw, and I didn't see the point in doing any spell work to focus them. Who wants to see all that anyway? So, I drink a tea. A special combination of herbs to suppress the power." I gasp in a breath, but the words keep tumbling out. "But it never got rid of the dreams. Most nights, I go to bed, and I see through Marbella's eyes. And she's always looking at you. Well, not *you*. She's looking at Henry. I think you might be a reincarnation of him."

I press my fingers to my lips to stop them from moving. Guilt and fear pound through me.

How could I?

Every crazy thing hovering, hidden between us, I just spewed out all at once.

Graham stares down at Marbella's picture, silent. Apparently, we've switched personalities this Mabon.

The sky has almost darkened completely, alerting the world to the end of another day.

Will this be our last full day together?

An image of us walking out of the woods teases my mind. We'll reach the car, and Graham will tell me he's calling a cab. He'll claim I've fabricated some obsessive story about him and declare he never wants to see me again.

I pray that the thought is a cruel trick of my brain and not a picture projected from the future, brought to me by my magic.

Chilly pinpricks on my cheek alert me that a few stray tears have started to trickle from the corners of my eyes. I hastily brush them away but not before Graham glances up and locks a surprised gaze on the movement.

"Fenny, no. Don't cry." And he's reaching for me, pulling me into his lap, comforting me with a kiss on my forehead and strong strokes down my spine.

Vulnerability has me burrowing into his chest, and it takes me a moment to realize he's shaking.

No, not shaking.

Laughing.

6

GRAHAM

She's a witch.

I'm in love with a witch, and my heart can barely handle the joy of that knowledge. All I can do is laugh.

Then, Fenella stares up at me with confusion, and I realize that during all of her confessing, she still hasn't told me she loves me. Some of my happiness drifts away.

But not my hope.

She's in my arms, and she just told me her secrets.

What better way to earn her love than to share my own?

"You're not the only one with magic," I whisper against her ear despite the fact that we're likely miles from any other living souls.

Fenella sits up straight so fast that she almost bludgeons my nose with her head. "You're a witch?" She clutches my face, as if the word might be tattooed on my forehead and she simply missed it these past six months.

"I don't know exactly what I am. Just that my family has always had a knack for plants."

"A knack for plants?" She deflates in my arms. "A green thumb isn't the same thing as magic, Graham."

My face aches from the grin that stretches across it. I never expected Fenella to be disappointed in the idea that I might *not* be magical.

Keeping one arm wrapped around her waist, I stretch out the other, letting my hand rest on the grass beside our blanket. "Just watch," I whisper.

In the twilight, our clearing has taken on a shadowy quality, and at first, the shift in the grass could be attributed to the flickering firelight. But when the stalks grow an inch, then another, and another, the change can't be denied.

Fenella gasps.

The tips of my fingers tingle and pulse with power. I redirect the energy to the trees. Branches above us extend and sprout extra leaves. Her eyes track the display, her lovely mouth open wide in shock.

Tired from the day's hike, I decide I've made my point and let the power trickle away. My arms ache as if I'd lifted weights, but that doesn't keep me from hugging Fenella close.

"I don't know any witch who can do that," she murmurs, her eyes glowing with fascination as they settle back on me.

"But witches can see the future?" That's one of the things I picked out of Fenella's uncharacteristically rapid confession.

She grimaces. "Witches have trouble using magic without the help of herbs, potions, and special words and symbols. I'll get flashes, random images. They could be past, present, or future. I'd have to put in a lot more effort if I wanted to knit them together. I'm not a very strong seer." Fenella fiddles with my shirt, pinching the thermal between her fingers.

"I'm not a seer at all, but I still had the dreams."

Fenella continues to watch her fidgeting hands. "What did you dream of exactly?"

"You." The answer comes immediately. Then, I remember

the portrait and amend my words. "Actually, Marbella, I guess. And the dreams are like scenes from a silent movie. Short. Quick. No sound at all."

She nods. "I don't think it has anything to do with seeing, although my dreams might be clearer because of my powers. I think they're memories we have because we're reincarnated."

"Reincarnated. What does that even mean?"

Fenella grimaces at the darkening tree line. "I've never been sure. I look like her. I see some of her memories. But is there any more of Marbella in me?"

She shrugs, and I realize my girlfriend is uncomfortable with the idea of being reincarnated. Can't say I'm totally at ease with it either. I decide to focus on a different line of questioning.

"Can you tell me what you know about them?"

Fenella hesitates but then tells me their story. A young woman coming upon a man ready to cut down a tree but stopping to talk to it instead. She paints me a picture of their many meetings that developed a strong romantic bond. Together, the two lovers explored the woods that cover the Blue Ridge Mountains. Marbella taught Henry about all the different plants and their medicinal uses while Henry showed Marbella how to approach skittish horses and how to set snares to catch rabbits and squirrels. Some of my own Henry memories pair up with her tales. Fenella smiles as she describes the house my ancestor planned to build for the two of them, a rustic cabin in the wilds of Virginia.

Then, she stops talking.

"What happened next?"

Fenella stares up at me, her eyes wide and uneasy. "I don't know."

"You never saw?"

She shakes her head. "The memories never go past a certain point in time. I don't see them older. And I ..."

I wait for her, feeling like something big is coming in her next words.

"I'm scared for them." She stares up at me with pleading eyes. "I'm scared for us."

Dread pools in my stomach. "Scared for us?"

Fenella reaches up, brushing her fingers through my beard as if to soothe me but also to assure herself I'm still here. "What if something bad happened to them? What if we're just playing out their relationship in modern time? What if that's what reincarnation is?"

I grasp her hands, holding them to my chest. "You can't know that."

"I can find out."

My eyebrows rise.

She pushes on. "Tonight is Mabon. The autumn equinox. One of the most powerful nights of the year for witches. I think I can utilize that power and this place and"—Fenella rests her forehead against mine—"you. With all that, I might be able to see what happened to them. Direct my visions to show me a certain time and place. Make sense of this." Desperation seeps into her voice.

I know, in this moment, without her speaking the words, that Fenella Henwood loves me.

But I also realize she won't admit that to herself without understanding the secrets of our shared past.

"Okay."

She jerks at my agreement, staring up at me with hope.

"Tell me what you need me to do."

Fenella rises from my lap, graceful, even as I notice her hands shaking with nerves.

"Build up the fire, please. I'll arrange everything else."

As I gather more branches, Fenella opens up a bundle I

didn't notice before. From it, she pulls out a hodgepodge of items and a small, worn book. After flipping to a certain page, she takes a moment to read whatever is written and then begins to arrange what I'm assuming are those special materials needed for casting spells.

I watch, fascinated, as she walks the perimeter of the clearing, setting down vibrant blue stones.

"What are those?"

"Lapis lazuli," she murmurs, distracted.

I keep quiet and let her work.

After we're enclosed in a circle of equally spaced stones, Fenella kneels in front of the tree that called to me earlier. From her bag, she pulls out a mason jar full of what looks like dirt. Unscrewing the lid, Fenella scatters the contents among the roots.

"Making an offering is important on Mabon," she explains while tucking the now-empty jar back in her bag.

The significance hits me, and I can't keep quiet any longer. "This is their spot. Where they first met."

Fenella walks toward me, nodding absently as she scans her spell book once more. "And that is their tree. You felt it, didn't you?" She glances at me over the fire.

Mutely, I nod, struck silent at the sight of her. Night fully upon us, the woman I love is illuminated solely by the firelight. She seems to glow, appearing wild and strong with her chestnut hair curling around her far-seeing eyes. Like a nymph from the forest, she moves with an unearthly grace, crouching by the flames and throwing in a handful of herbs that fill the air with delicious scents.

A tingling, like static electricity, kisses my skin. Strange shapes appear to dance in the blaze.

I blink to clear them from my eyes.

"You can sit back down. I'm almost done." Fenella's voice drifts in a distracted way, which makes me think part of her is somewhere else. The idea has me wanting to clutch her close, anchoring her here.

But I do as I was told, settling on our blanket with my back against a surprisingly warm stone.

She carefully replaces the book in her bag and retrieves one final item.

A flask.

Coming to kneel on the blanket, she offers me the first sip. The flavor of an earthy wine coats my tongue, leaving behind hints of herbs after I swallow.

She smiles. "You're too trusting. What if I were preparing you as a human sacrifice this whole time?"

I laugh, mainly from relief that even her half-dreamy state can still joke with me. "I'm happy to strip and spread out on an altar for you, if that's what you need."

Fenella gives me an evil grin before taking her own sip of the wine.

At this point, I expect her to sit across the fire from me and start chanting or maybe dance around the clearing and call out for guidance from the forest spirits.

Instead, Fenella crawls into my lap, situating herself between my legs, facing the aromatic flames.

"I usually get dizzy when I use my powers," she whispers. "Would you mind holding me steady?"

Glad for her permission, I wrap my arms around her, gathering her soft body against my chest. "I've got you."

She leans back with a sigh.

Slowly, the strange pressure in the clearing intensifies. The night itself seems to grow heavy, pressing down on my thoughts and worries.

And without realizing exactly what's happening, I find myself slipping into a shadowy corner of my own mind.

7

FENELLA

*T*he dream quality that normally infuses Marbella's memories is gone. As is the experience of me seeing through her eyes.

This scene in the forest isn't like all the others. Not some random piece of information plucked from my reincarnated soul.

This is my magic, directed by my spell work and infused with the power of Mabon.

"Where are we?" a hollow voice asks.

I whirl around to see Graham standing just behind me. My sudden movement did not ruffle a single leaf, nor break even the most fragile of twigs. My boyfriend hovers like a specter, wispy and insubstantial. I raise my hand to find I have as little consistency as he does.

"You're here?" My words sound like the tail end of an echo, fading into the darkening forest.

I hesitate to speak again, but Graham's baffled expression has me worried.

He might know magic exists in the world, but seeing into a true vision is much different than asking a plant to grow.

"The question isn't really *where*. It's *when*. And I'd guess about three hundred years ago."

"We time-traveled?" Graham tugs on his ear as if determined to pull it off his head.

Taking a step toward him, I offer my phantom hand in comfort. Expecting him to be at least a little scared of my vision form, I'm surprised when he immediately tugs me into his arms.

"This is a vision of the past. We're just watching it. Not really here," I explain, my head resting on a chest that is surprisingly firm despite its ghostly cast.

Emphasizing my point, Marbella passes by us. Graham tenses in my embrace, obviously just realizing we're not alone. But the woman paces around the clearing, not giving the slightest glance in our direction.

I examine the surroundings, trying to get our bearings, and realize we're standing in the same camping area we hiked to. Only none of our supplies are set up. The space is empty but for the young woman with my face nervously circling the perimeter. The time of day seems to be the conclusion of twilight, darkness quickly descending. A crude lantern hangs from a low branch, the light flickering, reflecting Marbella's anxious hand-ringing.

The sound of heavy footsteps causes her to pause. Graham and I turn to see who the newcomer is.

Henry emerges from the shadows, grinning in excitement, strolling up to Marbella with his arms spread wide. "My love, I have good news." Before saying anything else, he pulls her close and fits his mouth to hers.

The experience of seeing two people who look so much like my boyfriend and me kiss has my mind faltering.

Once they break apart, Marbella speaks first, "I have news too." Her voice, while breathless, holds no ounce of joy.

Henry doesn't seem to notice. "I must go first. I cannot

wait." He clasps her hands in his. "We finished the cabin today. Finally, there is a home I can give you. Tomorrow, I will go to your mother and ask for your hand."

Marbella's face loses what little color it had. Henry finally catches on that not all is well with his love.

"What is it, Bella? What is wrong?"

"We're leaving."

The couple stands silently for a moment while Graham and I watch whatever drama is about to unfold.

"Leaving?"

Marbella nods. "More people are settling in this area. And lately"—the woman breathes in deep—"there have been mutterings about witches."

Henry scowls. "Do they know?"

"Not yet. But some suspect. And that was all that was needed in Salem. My family isn't safe here. I am not safe here. So, we are leaving." Marbella retrieves her hands, fiddling with the fabric of her long skirt as she backs away from the man.

Henry lets out a sigh and tugs on his ear, gaze turned inward. After a moment, he speaks, "So be it. I will need a few days, maybe three, to make preparations."

Marbella shakes her head. "You are not coming."

"To hell I am not," he growls. "I love you, Bella. No matter where you go, I will follow."

"Your parents and your siblings need you."

"They've enough funds to hire help until my brother is grown."

"The journey is dangerous."

"A danger you plan to face without me?" Henry clasps Marbella's shoulders, pulling her to him, resting his forehead on hers. "We stay together. For the rest of our lives, we are partners."

The sigh that flows out of Marbella is full of sorrow. An ache begins in my heart, though I don't know why.

My ancestor reaches her hands up to cup Henry's bearded chin, and I watch a tear trail down a cheek the exact shape of mine. "I will love you until the day I die."

The magic comes quick and powerful, practically crackling through the air like lightning. That's when I notice the stones, equally spaced around the edge of the clearing. Lapis lazuli. Used to focus spells.

Marbella rises on her toes, pressing a gentle kiss to Henry's mouth and sliding her fingers up to rest on his temple.

"What is she doing?" Graham's question whispers through the thickening air.

Before I can voice my suspicions, Marbella speaks again, "I love you too much to subject you to my future." The young witch's voice cracks on the confession.

Her lover doesn't respond. Henry's eyes have drifted shut, his face gone slack.

"I am sorry."

The air grows heavy, swirling around the trees, tugging at Marbella's long skirts. The lovers' hair twists in the wind, the strands brushing together like grasping hands. Tension grows, as if large hands were bending an unforgiving branch until—

A snap. Loud as a thunderclap shaking the world.

The whirlwind settles, and the crackling air returns to a calm quiet.

When the witch eventually drops her hands and steps back, the last traces of magic dissipate.

Henry blinks and then stares around in confusion before settling his sights on Marbella. The horse farmer gazes at the woman he loves.

"Who are you?" he asks.

The horrible truth settles like rocks in my gut, and I turn to meet Graham's bewildered stare.

"She took his memories."

Then, the world goes black.

GRAHAM

When the world settles around us, we are back in the clearing, still in our phantom forms. The night has fully descended, but a mostly full moon sitting high in the night sky casts a white glow through the break in the canopy. I should be concerned with what we're about to see, but I'm still reeling from the discovery that Marbella erased herself from Henry's memory.

Why would she do that?

Her love for the man was clear in the way she cried for him.

If anything, the puzzle of the past has gotten more convoluted.

"Wh—"

"Shh." Fenella presses her mist-like fingers to my lips. "Someone is coming."

That's when I hear the uneven crunch of footsteps, and a moment later, Henry stumbles into the clearing.

But he seems off. Like he's drunk. Plus, he's barefoot and only wearing a long shirt.

"Come to me." Marbella's voice rings out, and suddenly, she's standing in the moonlight, her arms open.

I don't know how I missed her. She's too striking to have overlooked. Her curling hair hangs loose down her back, swaying in a breeze I cannot feel. All that covers her is an old-fashioned nightgown.

Henry strides forward, and I realize his eyes are closed, even as he moves.

The two lovers embrace, their mouths meeting, hands exploring.

As they strip each other, I can't help noticing how the pair differs from Fenella and myself. Their bodies are leaner, stronger, and show wear from a life lived hard.

Henry sinks to the ground, eyes still closed, and Marbella settles across his lap, sliding down onto his arousal. In the glow of the moon, the two of them make love, and my mind has trouble understanding the scene.

At times, it's like viewing a video of myself, and then there are moments when it seems like I'm being forced to watch some stranger fuck the woman I love.

Eventually, I turn to stare down at Fenella, needing to remember that whatever is playing out in front of us is not our story. Her gaze meets mine, full of discomfort. I give a rueful smile, and she rolls her eyes, nose wrinkling with her own suppressed humor.

A groan I've heard from my own throat plenty of times fills the woods.

Turning back, we find Marbella rising, leaving behind a sated partner.

For a moment, the man lies, panting on the ground.

When Henry sits up, he rubs his head, blinks his eyes open, and stares around the dark clearing as if waking from a dream. By this point, I'm used to not being seen in this vision place, but Henry's eyes pass over the woman he just slept with as if the space where she stands was empty. Marbella leans against a tree, seemingly unbothered by the lack of recognition.

The well-used man climbs to his feet and stumbles out of the clearing, leaving the three of us.

"She's not Marbella." Fenella's voice comes out whisper soft.

"Ah, so you have grasped who I am not. I will be truly impressed if you have discovered who I *am*."

We both give a startled jump at being addressed.

The woman who is not Marbella lets a smile play over her lips as she glances between us. "No guesses? How about now?"

A glow rises under her skin, blurring the features of Marbella's face. After a moment, the light fades, but it does not disappear completely. The visage left behind is different than any woman I've ever seen. Every angle of the face is sharper, longer, and yet the expression has a softness to it. I find that, as I attempt to study each feature, they blur. The only way I can look at the woman without getting dizzy is by letting my eyes relax and not trying too hard to actually *see* her.

"Modron?" Fenella speaks the name with a reverence that makes me feel like I'm missing something important.

The woman seems to smile. "Ah, The Mother. I have been called so before. But that is not all I am. I am also Earth. And … well, it almost seems vain to list every name humans and witches and elementals have given me."

"Elementals?" Fenella and I ask simultaneously.

The powerful figure waves her hand. "Descendants of the gods. Able to manipulate the world around them. Like you, my child." Her eerie focus rests on me.

I flinch. "You're not my mother."

The chuckle she lets flow sounds like birds chirping. "No. But you do come from me. From this." Her long fingers point to the space of grass flattened by the recent tryst.

"I don't understand," Fenella speaks my thoughts.

The woman, Earth, sighs. "Of course. It is all out of order for you." She saunters around the clearing, trailing her fingers along trees as she moves, leaving each plant with a healthy glow. "Henry was a man after my own heart. He showed respect to all my creations. And the day he found love in my woods, I danced in celebration. But Marbella was young and powerful, and"—the deity lets out a soul-suffering sigh—"she peered into the future, hoping to find happiness. Instead, she saw her death."

Fenella gasps, and I pull her ghostly form into me, fear spiking through my insubstantial body.

Earth gives a sorrowful nod. "Such a waste. Dying young. Of course, that future did not have to come to pass. There were many other futures open to her. But, somewhere, the witches lost that knowledge. That visions of the future are barely better than guesses." The figure shrugs her glimmering shoulders. "So, Marbella decided she would be the only one to suffer. She would take away Henry's love for her, and he could live a long life without her.

"That day, I did not dance. That day, I wept."

"But what does this have to do with us?" Fenella's fingers tangle in my shirt as she addresses the magical figure.

"Marbella destroyed Henry's memories, but their love was stronger than any spell. After their deaths, that love survived. Two souls seeking each other throughout time, waiting for new bodies to fit into. But not just any bodies. There needed to be a blood connection to the original vessels. Marbella died young, like she had seen. She rescued her younger sister from a flash flood during their travels but was not able to save herself. You, Fenella, are descended from Marbella's sister."

The strength of the woman's gaze settles back on me. "Henry's line, however, was at risk. His siblings passed before reaching adulthood, and though he eventually married, his wife was barren. I walked in these woods beside him, watching the years crease his fragile human body. And I despaired for the love that still beat strong, hidden deep in his heart. So, on Mabon night, I wore Marbella's face and gave him a living dream. He did not know why he longed for the woman, only that the joining filled a dark place in his soul. I left the child on their doorstep, and the barren wife rejoiced at the chance to be a mother."

"I'm not sure Marbella would thank you for sleeping with the man she loved," Fenella mutters, and I don't know whether to chuckle or shield her from possible retaliation.

"If I had not, you would be lacking a circle of arms to stand in at the moment." Earth offers the comment without heat, but Fenella hugs me close, as if the woman might snatch me from her.

I press a reassuring kiss to my love's forehead.

"So, what are we then? Just copies of Marbella and Henry? Do we even have a choice?"

I flinch at her words. *Is this what weighs on her? The idea that she loves me for no other reason than the fact that we are reincarnations?*

Earth reaches up to fiddle with a leaf, not plucking it, just caressing it. "Marbella and Henry are dead. They left this plane of existence long ago. All that is left is a piece of each. You have your own souls and a bit of theirs. Their love. But I ask, is love all that is needed to find a partner? There are those who love but do not quite like one another. There are those who share a strange, twisted love and spend their days hurting each other. There are those who love, but the lives they seek to live do not fit, and so their affection sours and curdles into resentment. If Marbella and Henry's love feels foreign, uncomfortable, like a sickness in your soul"— suddenly, the woman is standing in front of us both, one of her overly warm palms pressed to each of our chests—"I'll free you of it."

Before I can even comprehend what Earth is offering,

Fenella lashes out, shoving the mystical being away with something bordering on violence. "No! Don't," she pants, eyes wild. "Don't make him stop loving me!"

My determined witch braces herself in front of me, a wall between what I'm almost certain is a god and myself. I rest my hands on Fenella's waist, ready to pull her out of the way if necessary.

Earth grins, clearly satisfied with Fenella's reaction. "I have acted as the protector of their souls for centuries. I did not pass them to you to relieve myself of a burden. They were a gift. One you never had to accept. I asked your sweet Daisy to help with an introduction. After that, all choices were yours. They always will be." A sadness drifts off the woman, a sense of regret. "Marbella and Henry filled my forest with their love once, and they deserved more time. Fear of the future has killed many promising romances. I hope you do not become another set of casualties."

Earth turns her back on us, her body shimmering and dissipating as she strolls toward the shadows between the trees. In fact, the whole scene seems to be evaporating around us, and I tug Fenella back into my arms, needing her close.

Just before darkness descends, a final comment floats to us.

"What is a life without love?"

8

FENELLA

"*F*enella? Fenny? Can you open your eyes for me? I'm freaking out a little bit here."

A heavy weight lifts from my brain, and I blink, finding myself staring up at a worried Graham. When our eyes meet, his handsome face creases in a relieved smile, crinkling his copper beard.

"You were there." The words croak out of my throat, and I turn my head fast to keep from coughing in his face.

A moment later, the mouth of a water bottle is pressed to my lips. I drink deep. The residue of magic clears as I swallow.

"I guess that was all real then. Not some fever dream," Graham muses while helping me sit up straight.

Our fire is low, and the woods are fully dark. The night of the autumn equinox is upon us.

And with it, a balance seems to have righted itself.

"It wasn't a dream. Every second of it was real." I turn in his hold, reaching up to cup his cheeks in my hands.

Love flows through me, and for the first time, I don't question it.

In that moment, when Earth threatened to remove our connection, I knew that even if the love had once been Marbella's, it was mine now. I claim it, and I claim Graham. Nothing, not even a goddess, will take him away from me.

"I love you, Graham."

His throat bobs with a deep swallow, and a spark that has nothing to do with flickering firelight blazes in his gaze. "You do?"

My lips tilt at the corners as I enjoy the hope in his question. "I'm sorry I didn't say it sooner. I just wanted to know the words were mine, not Marbella's. But I do know. *I love you.*"

"Thank the goddess," he mutters a second before pressing his mouth to mine.

We fold ourselves together, basking in our love under a night sky bright with stars, surrounded by a forest humming with hushed melodies of magic.

ACKNOWLEDGMENTS

This may have been a small project, but I still appreciate the people who helped me get it ready for the autumn equinox. Thank you Blair and Anna for beta reading, and thank you Sylwia for your encouraging words. Jovana, you are a fantastic editor and always help my books end up as something readable.

I also want to thank everyone who reads this little story. I hope your lives are full of adorable dogs, ripe pumpkins, and magic!

ABOUT THE AUTHOR

Lauren Connolly works as an academic librarian when she's not crafting love stories. This means she's used to researching random topics—from revitalizing rural communities in Japan to the stigma held against horse slaughter and consumption in the United States. (That last one was a bit difficult, what with her being a vegetarian, but she did it!)

In her free time, Lauren wrestles with her grumpy cocker spaniel, named after her favorite pop culture librarian; drives or flies long distances to visit family and friends around the world; reminds herself she should do something healthy, like lift weights or yoga; and stays up past her bedtime to read "just one more page."

Join her newsletter.

ALSO BY LAUREN CONNOLLY

You Only Need One